LINCOLN
& Other

By
EDWIN MARKHAM

Note

Many of the poems in this volume now appear in print for the first time. The one on Lincoln was read at the Lincoln Birthday Dinner given in by the Republican Club of New York City. The poem "The New Century" was read at the Manhattan Labor Dinner given January first, .

Edwin Markham.
West New Brighton
New York
LINCOLN &
OTHER POEMS

Lincoln, the Man of the People

When the Norn-Mother saw the Whirlwind Hour,
Greatening and darkening as it hurried on,
She bent the strenuous Heavens and came down
To make a man to meet the mortal need.
She took the tried clay of the common road—
Clay warm yet with the genial heat of Earth,
Dashed through it all a strain of prophecy;
Then mixed a laughter with the serious stuff.
It was a stuff to wear for centuries,
A man that matched the mountains, and compelled
The stars to look our way and honor us.
The color of the ground was in him, the red earth;
The tang and odor of the primal things—
The rectitude and patience of the rocks;
The gladness of the wind that shakes the corn;
The courage of the bird that dares the sea;
The justice of the rain that loves all leaves;
The pity of the snow that hides all scars;
The loving-kindness of the wayside well;
The tolerance and equity of light
That gives as freely to the shrinking weed
As to the great oak flaring to the wind—

To the grave's low hill as to the Matterhorn
That shoulders out the sky.
And so he came.
From prairie cabin up to Capitol,
One fair Ideal led our chieftain on.
Forevermore he burned to do his deed
With the fine stroke and gesture of a king.
He built the rail-pile as he built the State,
Pouring his splendid strength through every blow,
The conscience of him testing every stroke,
To make his deed the measure of a man.
So came the Captain with the mighty heart:
And when the step of Earthquake shook the house,
Wrenching the rafters from their ancient hold,
He held the ridgepole up, and spiked again
The rafters of the Home. He held his place—
Held the long purpose like a growing tree—
Held on through blame and faltered not at praise.
And when he fell in whirlwind, he went down
As when a kingly cedar green with boughs
Goes down with a great shout upon the hills,
And leaves a lonesome place against the sky.

In a Corn-field

Who was it passed me, his body a-throbbing?
Who but Sir Humblebee home from his robbing!
What is that crackle of chariots whirling?
'Tis Cricket Achilles where green smoke is curling.
And who is it comes on the bloom-ocean steering?
Bold Dragonfly Cortez, a-tacking and veering!

The Sower

Written after seeing Millet's painting with this title
Soon will the lonesome cricket by the stone
Begin to hush the night; and lightly blown
Field fragrances will fill the fading blue—

Old furrow-scents that ancient Eden knew.
Soon in the upper twilight will be heard
The winging whisper of a homing bird.
Who is it coming on the slant brown slope,
Touched by the twilight and her mournful hope—
Coming with hero step, with rhythmic swing,
Where all the bodily motions weave and sing?
The grief of the ground is in him, yet the power
Of Earth to hide the furrow with the flower.
He is the stone rejected, yet the stone
Whereon is built metropolis and throne.
Out of his toil come all their pompous shows,
Their purple luxury and plush repose!
The grime of this bruised hand keeps tender white
The hands that never labor, day nor night.
His feet that know only the field's rough floors
Send lordly steps down echoing corridors.
Yea, this vicarious toiler at the plow
Gives that fine pallor to my lady's brow.
And idle armies with their boom and blare,
Flinging their foolish glory on the air—
He hides their nakedness, he gives them bed,
And by his alms their hungry mouths are fed.
Not his the lurching of an aimless clod,
For with the august gesture of a god—
A gesture that is question and command—
He hurls the bread of nations from his hand;
And in the passion of the gesture flings
His fierce resentment in the face of kings.
This is the Earth-god of the latter day,
Treading with solemn joy the upward way;
A lusty god that in some crowning hour
Will hurl Gray Privilege from the place of power.
These are the inevitable steps that make
Unreason tremble and Tradition shake.
This is the World-Will climbing to its goal,
The climb of the unconquerable Soul—
Democracy whose sure insurgent stride

Jars kingdoms to their ultimate stone of pride.

At Little Virgil's Window

There are three green eggs in a small brown pocket,
And the breeze will swing and the gale will rock it,
Till three little birds on the thin edge teeter,
And our God be glad and our world be sweeter!

The Muse of Brotherhood

I am in the Expectancy that runs:
My feet are in the Future, whirled afar
On wings of light. If I have any sons,
Let them arise and follow to my star.
Some momentary touches of my fire
Have warmed the barren ages with a beam:
There is no peak beyond my swift desire,
There is no beauty deeper than my dream.
I make an end of life's stupendous jest—
The merry waste of fortunes by the Few,
While the thin faces of the poor are pressed
Against the panes—a hungry whirlwind crew.
I come to lift the soul-destroying weight,
To heal the hurt, to end the foolish loss,
To take the toiler from his brutal fate—
The toiler hanging on the Labor Cross.
I bring to Earth the feel of home again,
That men may nestle on her warm, still breast;
I bring to wronged, humiliated men
The sacred right to labor and to rest.
I bring to men the fine ideal stuff
The young gods took to build the spheres of old:
The fire I send on men is great enough
To burn the iron kingdoms into gold.
I hold the way until the bright heavens bend—
Until the New Republic shall arise,
And quick young deities again descend,

Bringing the gifts of God with joyous cries.
I lead the Graces and the Wingèd Powers:
The world the Anarchs build I will destroy,
For I will storm upon its demon towers,
With wind of laughter and with rain of joy.
And at the first break of my Social Song
A hush will fall upon the foolish strife,
As though a joyous god, serene and strong,
Shined suddenly before the steps of life.
Cold hearts that falter are my only bar:
Heroes that seek my ever-fading goal
Must take their reckoning from the central star,
And follow the equator: I am Soul.
My love is higher than heavens where Taurus wheels,
My love is deeper than the pillared skies:
High as that peak in Heaven where Milton kneels,
Deep as that grave in Hell where Cæsar lies.
Still hope for man: my star is on the way!
Great Hugo saw it from his prison isle;
It lit the mighty dream of Lamennais;
It led the ocean thunders of Carlyle.
Wise Greeley saw the star of my desire,
Wise Lincoln knelt before my hidden flame:
It was from me they drew their sacred fire—
I am Religion by her deeper name.

A Blossoming Bough

A blossoming bough against the sky,
And all my blood is aleap with life,
As though glad violins went by
In wild delicious strife!
And the Suisun Hills again are green!
And I am a boy in the canyons deep,
Where the gray sycamores flicker and lean,
And waters plunge and sleep.
A light, quick wind blows into my heart,
Faint with the breath of apple trees;

And my lyric lark is back with a start—
And orchards like white seas!

Kyka

Child-heart!
Wild heart!
What can I bring you,
What can I sing you,
You who have come from a glory afar,
Called into Time from a secret star?
Fleet one!
Sweet one!
Whose was the wild hand
Shaped you in child-land,
Framing the flesh with a flash of desire,
Pouring the soul as a fearful fire?
Strong child!
Song child!
Who can unravel
All your long travel
Out of the Mystery, birth after birth—
Out of the dim worlds deeper than Earth?
Mad thing!
Glad thing!
How will Life tame you?
How will God name you?
All that I know is that you are to me
Wind over water, star on the sea.
Dear heart!
Near heart!
Long is the journey,
Hard is the tourney:
Would I could be by your side when you fall—
Would that my own heart could suffer it all!

A Mendocino Memory

Once in my lonely, eager youth I rode,
With jingling spur, into the clouds' abode—
Rode northward lightly as the high crane goes—
Rode into the hills in the month of the frail wild rose,
To find the soft-eyed heifers in the herds,
Strayed north along the trail of nesting birds,
Following the slow march of the springing grass,
From range to range, from pass to flowering pass.
I took the trail: the fields were yet asleep;
I saw the last star hurrying to its deep—
Saw the shy wood-folk starting from their rest
In many a crannied rock and leafy nest.
A bold, tail-flashing squirrel in a fir,
Restless as fire, set all the boughs astir;
A jay, in dandy blue, flung out a fine
First fleering sally from a sugar-pine.
A flight of hills, and then a deep ravine
Hung with madrono boughs—the quail's demesne;
A quick turn in the road, a wingèd whir,
And there he came with fluted whispering,
The captain of the chaparral, the king,
With nodding plume, with circumstance and stir,
And step of Carthaginian conqueror!
I climbed the canyon to a river-head,
And looking backward saw a splendor spread,
Miles beyond miles, of every kingly hue
And trembling tint the looms of Arras knew—
A flowery pomp as of the dying day,
A splendor where a god might take his way.
And farther on the wide plains under me,
I watched the light-foot winds of morning go,
Soft shading over wheat-fields far and free,
To keep their old appointment with the sea.
And farther yet, dim in the distant glow,
Hung on the east a line of ghostly snow.
After the many trails an open space
Walled by the tulès of a perished lake;
And there I stretched out, bending the green brake,

And felt it cool against my heated face.
My horse went cropping by a sunny crag,
In wild oats taller than the antlered stag
That makes his pasture there. In gorge below
Blind waters pounded boulders, blow on blow—
Waters that gather, scatter and amass
Down the long canyons where the grizzlies pass,
Slouching through manzanita thickets old,
Strewing the small red apples on the ground,
Tearing the wild grape from its tree-top hold,
And wafting odors keen through all the hills around.
Now came the fording of the hurling creeks,
And joyous days among the breezy peaks,
Till through the hush of many canyons fell
The faint quick tenor of a brazen bell,
A sudden, soft, hill-stilled, far-falling word,
That told the secret of the straying herd.
It was the brink of night, and everywhere
Tall redwoods spread their filmy tops in air;
Huge trunks, like shadows upon shadow cast,
Pillared the under twilight, vague and vast.
And one had fallen across the mountain way,
A tree hurled down by hurricane to lie
With torn-out roots pronged-up against the sky
And clutching still their little dole of clay.
Lightly I broke green branches for a bed,
And gathered ferns, a pillow for my head.
And what to this were kingly chambers worth—
Sleeping, an ant, upon the sheltering earth,
High over Mendocino's windy capes,
Where ships go flying south like shadow-shapes—
Gleam into vision and go fading on,
Bearing the pines hewn out of Oregon.

The Witness of the Dust

Voices are crying from the dust of Tyre,
From Baalbec and the stones of Babylon—

"We raised our pillars upon Self-Desire,
And perished from the large gaze of the sun."
Eternity was on the pyramid,
And immortality on Greece and Rome;
But in them all the ancient Traitor hid,
And so they tottered like unstable foam.
There was no substance in their soaring hopes:
The voice of Thebes is now a desert cry;
A spider bars the road with filmy ropes,
Where once the feet of Carthage thundered by.
A bittern booms where once fair Helen laughed;
A thistle nods where once the Forum poured;
A lizard lifts and listens on a shaft,
Where once of old the Colosseum roared.
No house can stand, no kingdom can endure
Built on the crumbling rock of Self-Desire:
Nothing is Living Stone, nothing is sure,
That is not whitened in the Social Fire.

The Wall Street Pit

I see a hell of faces surge and whirl,
Like maelstrom in the ocean—faces lean
And fleshless as the talons of a hawk—
Hot faces like the faces of the wolves
That track the traveler fleeing through the night—
Grim faces shrunken up and fallen in,
Deep-plowed like weather-eaten bark of oak—
Drawn faces like the faces of the dead,
Grown suddenly old upon the brink of Earth.
Is this a whirl of madmen ravening,
And blowing bubbles in their merriment?
Is Babel come again with shrieking crew
To eat the dust and drink the roaring wind?
And all for what? A handful of bright sand
To buy a shroud with and a length of earth?
Oh, saner are the hearts on stiller ways!
Thrice happier they who, far from these wild hours,

Grow softly as the apples on a bough.
Wiser the plowman with his scudding blade,
Turning a straight fresh furrow down a field—
Wiser the herdsman whistling to his heart,
In the long shadows at the break of day—
Wiser the fisherman with quiet hand,
Slanting his sail against the evening wind.
The swallow sweeps back from the south again,
The green of May is edging all the boughs,
The shy arbutus glimmers in the wood,
And yet this hell of faces in the town—
This storm of tongues, this whirlpool roaring on,
Surrounded by the quiets of the hills;
The great calm stars forever overhead,
And, under all, the silence of the dead!
May, .

A Creed

To Mr. David Lubin
There is a destiny that makes us brothers:
None goes his way alone:
All that we send into the lives of others
Comes back into our own.
I care not what his temples or his creeds,
One thing holds firm and fast—
That into his fateful heap of days and deeds
The soul of a man is cast.

The Mighty Hundred Years

I

I saw the Muses, in august assize,
Standing before the Planetary Norns,
Their faces lit with calm, victorious eyes,
Weird as the beauty shed on starry morns.
I heard a voice cry from the Judgment Seat:

"Declare unto the Rulers of the Spheres
The story of the triumph and defeat,
The story of The Mighty Hundred Years."
And then the Muses, bearing in their hands
High sibylline scrolls, sang to the Sceptered Powers:
"The sun ascends in man, the sky expands;
Into the Comrade-Future climb the Hours.
"The dawn was loud with thunders, white with levin,
Walled by the whirlwind, dark with agèd wrong;
Then came the bright steps of the Lyric Seven,
And heights and depths grew resonant with song.
"Above the dead the circling music sprang—
Dead custom, dead religion, dead desire;
Down the keen wind of dawn the rapture rang,
White with new dream and shot with Shelley's fire.
"Out of the whirlwind Truth that came on France,
Rose the young Titaness, Democracy,
Superb in gesture, with the godlike glance;
Now stirred, now still with dream of things to be.
"She drew all faces as a lighted tower,
Strong mother of men, molded of lion race;
And all men's hearts were shaken by her power,
The strange, disturbing beauty of her face.
"New seeing came upon the eyes of men,
New life ran pulsing in the veins of Earth:
It was a sifting of the souls again,
The weighing of the ages and their worth.
II

"Man burst the chains that his own hands had made;
Hurled down the blind, fierce gods that in blind years
He fashioned, and a power upon them laid
To bruise his heart and shake his soul with fears.
"He peered through nature, peered into the past,
Careless of hoary precedent and pact;
And sworn to know the truth of things at last,
Knelt at the altar of the Naked Fact.
"One mighty gleam, and old horizons broke!

All the vast, glimmering outline of the Whole
Swam on the vision, shifting, at one stroke,
The ancient gravitation of the soul.
"All things came circling in one cosmic dance,
One motion older than the ages are;
Swung by one Law, one Purpose, one Advance,
Serene and steadfast as the morning star.
"And now men trace the orbits of the Law,
And find it is their shelter and their friend;
For there, behind its mystery and awe,
God's sure hand presses to a blessèd end.
"So man is climbing toward the Secret Vast—
Up through the storm of stars, skies upon skies;
And down through circling atoms, nearing fast
The brink of things, beyond which Chaos lies.
"Yea, in the shaping of a grain of sand,
He sees the law that made the spheres to be—
Sees atom-worlds spun by the Hidden Hand,
To whirl about their small Alcyone.
"With spell of wizard Science on his eyes,
And augment on his arm, he probes through space;
Or pushes back the low, unfriendly skies,
To feel the wind of Saturn on his face.
"He walks abroad upon the Zodiac,
To weigh the worlds in balances, to fuse
Suns in his crucible, and carry back
The spheral music and the cosmic news.

III

"And now the Powers of Water, Fire, and Air,
And that dread Thing behind the lightning's light
Cry, Master us, O man, for thou art fair;
To serve thee is our freedom and our might.
"We love the craft that found our hidden place—
The beauty of the cunning of thy hands;
We love the quiet empire of thy face:
Hook us with steel and harness us with bands!

"Make us the Genius of the crookèd plow;
The Spirit in the whisper of the wheels;
The unseen Presence sitting at the prow,
To urge the wanderings huge, sea-cleaving keels.
"They come from ocean and the sun's blue tent;
He lays bright harness on them, and his word;
New pulse from continent to continent
Runs; the dead places of the world are stirred.
"Bearing the sceptres of the mystery,
Man rides at elbow with the flying gale,
Shrinks up the ancient spaces: land and sea
Dispute his wingèd way without avail—
"All but the Arctic silences, where stands
The Spirit of the Winters, and denies,
With incontestable gesture of white hands,
And lure of baleful beauty in her eyes.
"It is the hour of man: new Purposes,
Broad-shouldered, press against the world's slow gate;
And voices from the vast eternities
Still preach the soul's austere apostolate.
"Always there will be vision for the heart,
The press of endless passion: every goal
A traveler's tavern, whence he must depart
On new divine adventures of the soul."

Which Was Dream?

Suggested by an ancient Chinese classic
I thought that I dreamed a dream one night—
That I was a moth on a joyous flight,
Under a sky the west wind cools,
Over a sky of fields and pools.
Like a tinted leaf in the wind content,
Over a wonderful world I went:
Over a valley with wavering wing
My shadow flew like a startled thing.
On through the waters spread below,
I saw my delicate phantom go—

On, till a flash, and that bright world broke,
And I was a man at a sudden stroke!
And now a wonder is on my heart
Of that world that went at a sudden start—
Of this world that came at a stroke of hand,
Hung under stars at some high command!
For now I never can surely know
Whether in deed or in dream I go;
Whether I was in that other sky
Only a dream-moth straying by;
Or whether that world was the world of truth
And this one only a dream forsooth;
Whether perchance for a little span
A moth is not dreaming itself a man!

Our Deathless Dead

How shall we honor them, our Deathless Dead?
With strew of laurel and the stately tread?
With blaze of banners brightening overhead?
Nay, not alone these cheaper praises bring:
They will not have this easy honoring.
Not all our cannon, breaking the blue noon,
Not the rare reliquary, writ with rune,
Not all the iterance of our reverent cheers,
Not all sad bugles blown,
Can honor them grown saintlier with the years.
Nor can we praise alone
In the majestic reticence of stone:
Not even our lyric tears
Can honor them, passed upward to their spheres.
Nay, we must meet our august hour of fate
As they met theirs; and this will consecrate,
This honor them, this stir their souls afar,
Where they are climbing to an ampler star.
The soaring pillar and the epic boast,
The flaring pageant and the storied pile
May parley with Oblivion awhile,

To save some Sargon of the fading host;
But these are vain to hold
Against the slow creep of the patient mold,
The noiseless drill of the erasing rust:
The pomp, the arch, the scroll cannot beguile
The ever-circling Destinies that must
Mix king and clown into one rabble dust.
No name of mortal is secure in stone:
Hewn on the Parthenon, the name will waste;
Carved on the Pyramid, 'twill be effaced.
In the heroic deed and there alone,
Is man's one hold against the craft of Time,
That humbles into dust the shaft sublime—
That mixes sculptured Karnak with the sands,
unannealed, blown about the Libyan lands.
And for the high, heroic deeds of men,
There is no crown of praise but deed again.
Only the heart-quick praise, the praise of deed,
Is faithful praise for the heroic breed.
How shall we honor them, our Deathless Dead?
How keep their mighty memories alive?
In him who feels their passion, they survive!
Flatter their souls with deed, and all is said!
In the heroic soul their souls create
Is raised remembrance past the reach of fate.
The will to serve and bear,
The will to love and dare,
And take for God unprofitable risk—
These things, these things will utter praise and pæan
Louder than lyric thunders Æschylean;
These things will build our dead unwasting obelisk.

The Builders

I dwell near a murmur of leaves,
And my labor is sweeter than rest;
For over my head in the shade of the eaves
A throstle is building his nest.

And he teaches me gospels of joy,
As he gurgles and shouts in his toil:
It is brimming with rapture, his wild employ,
Bearing a straw for spoil.
So I know 'twas a joyous God
Who stretched out the splendor of things,
And gave to my bird the cool green sod,
A sky, and a venture of wings.
But why are my brothers so still?
They are building a lordly hall—
They are building a palace there on the hill,
But there's never a song in it all!

The Angelus

Suggested by Millet's painting with this title
Far through the lilac sky the Angelus bell
Brings back again the hail of Gabriel.
Its refluent, three-fold, immemorial rhyme
Follows the fading sun, from clime to clime—
Ripples and lives a moment in the heart,
Wherever the dark hours come and the bright depart.
From land to fading land, the whole world round,
It airily runs, a rosary of sound—
Bursts silverly on sainted Palestine;
Lives for a moment on the Apennine;
Flings on the fields of France a far refrain;
Sends a sweet trouble on the bells of Spain;
Touches Manhattan; hurries on to be
A murmur on Saint Francis by the sea.
But dreamily here the hours of evening go,
With tented haycocks in the rosy glow—
Gray heaps that Homer saw in ages gone,
Sweet-smelling heaps that Abel rested on.
And two have heard the summons on the air,
And turned from labor, the embodied prayer;
Bowed with the fine humility of trees,
Of bended barley in the quiet breeze;

As faithful as the never-failing Earth
That gives us bread of rest and bread of mirth;
As patient as the rocks that have been still
Since put into their places on the hill;
In league with Earth and all her quiet things,
Whose lives are wrapped in shade and whisperings;
In league with Earth and all the things that live
To give their toil for others and forgive.
Pausing to let the hush of evening pass
Across the soul, as shadow over grass,
They cease their day-long sacrament of toil,
That living prayer, the tilling of the soil!
And richer are their two-fold worshippings
Than flare of pontiff or the pomp of kings.
For each true deed is worship: it is prayer,
And carries its own answer unaware.
Yes, they whose feet upon good errands run
Are friends of God, with Michael of the sun;
Yes, each accomplished service of the day
Paves for the feet of God a lordlier way.
The souls that love and labor through all wrong,
They clasp His hand and make the circle strong;
They lay the deep foundation, stone by stone,
And build into Eternity God's throne!
He is more pleased by some sweet human use
Than by the learnèd book of the recluse;
Sweeter are comrade kindnesses to Him
Than the high harpings of the Seraphim;
More than white incense circling to the dome
Is a field well furrowed or a nail sent home.
More than the hallelujahs of the choirs
Or hushed adorings at the altar fires,
Is a loaf well kneaded or a room swept clean
With light-heart love that finds no labor mean.

The Suicide

Toil-worn, and trusting Zeno's mad belief,

A soul went wailing from the world of grief:
A wild hope led the way,
Then suddenly—dismay!
Lo, the old load was There—
The duty, the despair!
Nothing had changed: still only one escape
From its old self into the angel shape.

The Ascension

Mary Magdalene telleth to the family at Bethany the Story of the Ascension
In the gray dawn they left Jerusalem,
And I rose up to follow after them.
He led toward Bethany by the narrow bridge
Of Kedron, upward to the olive ridge.
Once on the camel path beyond the City,
He looked back, struck at heart with pain and pity—
Looked backward from the two lone cedar trees
On Olivet, alive to every breeze—
Looked in a rush of sudden tears, and then
Went steadily on, never to turn again.
Near the green quiets of a little wood
The Master halted silently and stood.
The figs were purpling, and a fledgling dove
Had fallen from a windy bough above,
And lay there crying feebly by a thorn,
Its little body bruisèd and forlorn.
He stept aside a moment from the rest
And put it safely back into the nest.
Then mighty words did seem to rise in Him
And die away: even as white vapors swim
A moment on Mount Carmel's purple steep,
And then are blown back rainless to the deep.
And once He looked up with a little start:
Perhaps some loved name passed across His heart,
Some memory of a road in Galilee,
Or old familiar rock beside the Sea.

And suddenly there broke upon our sight
A rush of angels terrible with light—
The high same host the Shepherds saw go by,
Breaking the starry night with lyric cry—
A rush of angels, wistful and aware,
That shook a thousand colors on the air—
Colors that made a music to the eye—
Glories of lilac, azure, gold, vermilion,
Blown from the air-hung delicate pavilion.
And now His face grew bright with luminous will:
The great grave eyes grew planet-like and still.
Yea, in that moment all His face fire-white
Seemed struck out of imperishable light.
Delicious apprehension shook the spirit,
With song so still that only the heart could hear it.
A sense of something sacred, starry, vast,
Greater than Earth, across the being passed.
Then with a stretching of His hands to bless,
A last unspeakable look that was caress,
Up through the vortice of bright cherubim
He rose until the august form grew dim—
Up through the blue dome of the day ascended,
By circling flights of seraphim befriended.
He was uplifted from us, and was gone
Into the darkness of another dawn.

All-Men's Inn

Death is the only host with thoughts so large
He cannot find it in his heart to charge.
He turns no guest away: madame and sir,
This inn has bed for every traveller.
I'll meet you, emperor—I'll meet you, clown,
At this last tavern as we leave the town.

The Field Fraternity

When God's warm justice is revealed—

The Kingdom that the Father planned—
His children all will equal stand
As trees upon a level field.
There each one has a goodly space—
Each yeoman of the woodland race—
Each has a foothold on the Earth,
A place for business and for mirth.
No privilege bars a tree's access
To Earth's whole store of preciousness.
The trees stand level on God's floor,
With equal nearness to His store.
And trees, they have no private ends,
But stand together as close friends.
They send their beauty on all things,
An equal gift to clowns and kings.
They worry not: there is enough
Laid by for them of God's good stuff—
Enough for all, and so no fear
Sends boding on their blameless cheer.
So from the field comes curious news—
That each one takes what it can use—
Takes what its lifted arms can hold
Of sky-sweet rain and beamy gold;
And all give back with pleasure high
Their riches to the sun and sky.
Yes, since the first star they have stood
A testament of Brotherhood.

The Errand Imperious

Proud England brooding on the days to come—
Mother of peoples and of song undying—
Hears in all lands the doubling of her drum,
Sees on all winds of the world her lone flag flying.
And Russia, young, barbaric in her power,
With untried tendons, cramped in all her length,
Chafing in snowy lair, dreams of the hour
When she shall loose on Earth her hairy strength.

And Germany, whose blonde intrepid might
Once sent her Saxon fire on every land,
Hears the great Labor Angel down the night,
Crying, "Behold, my judgments are at hand!"
And elder kingdoms by the Midland Sea,
Whose every crag has burned with battle fire,
Feel the young pulses of the days to be,
And hear far voices call them to aspire.
But harken, my America, my own,
Great Mother, with the hill-flower in your hair!
Diviner is that light you bear alone,
That dream that keeps your face forever fair.
Imperious is your errand and sublime,
And that which binds you is Orion's band.
For some large Purpose, since the youth of Time,
You were kept hidden in the Lord's right hand.
You were kept hidden in a secret place,
With white Sierras, white Niagaras—
Hid under stalwart stars in this far space,
Ages ere Tadmor or the man of Uz.
'Tis yours to bear the World-State in your dream,
To strike down Mammon and his brazen breed,
To build the Brother-Future, beam on beam;
Yours, mighty one, to shape the Mighty Deed.
The armèd heavens lean down to hear your fame,
America: rise to your high-born part!
The thunders of the sea are in your name,
The splendors and the terrors in your heart.

Love's To-Morrow

For Florence Sharon
Ease of heart or ache of heart,
Tell me, Love, the thing to be:
Flower of dream or dust of dream,
You can choose the one for me.
Fire or ash of fire, who knows?
Both are folded in the flame.

Life all grey and life all rose
Are hidden in your name.
January, .

The Leader of the People

Swung in the Purpose of the upper sphere,
We sweep on to the century anear.
But something makes the heart of man forebode:
There is a new Sphinx watching by the road!
Its name is Labor, and the world must hear—
Must hear and answer its dread Question—yea,
Or perish as the tribes of yesterday.
Thunder and Earthquake crouch beyond the gate;
But fear not: man is greater than his fate.
For one will come with Answer—with a word
Wherein the whole world's gladness shall be heard;
One who will feel the grief in every breast,
The heart-cry of humanity for rest.
So we await the Leader to appear,
Lover of men, thinker and doer and seer,
The hero who will fill the labor throne
And build the Comrade Kingdom, stone by stone;
That kingdom that is greater than the Dream
Breaking through ancient vision, gleam by gleam—
Something that Song alone can faintly feel,
And only Song's wild rapture can reveal.
Thrilled by the Cosmic Oneness he will rise,
Youth in his heart and morning in his eyes;
While glory fallen from the far-off goal
Will send mysterious splendor on his soul.
Him shall all toilers know to be their friend;
Him shall they follow faithful to the end.
Though every leaf were a tongue to cry, "Thou must!"
He will not say the unjust thing is just.
Not all the fiends that curse in the eclipse
Shall shake his heart or hush his lyric lips.
His cry for justice, it will stir the stones

From Hell's black granite to the seraph thrones!
Earth listens for the coming of his feet;
The hushed Fates lean expectant from their seat.
He will be calm and reverent and strong,
And, carrying in his words the fire of song,
Will send a hope upon these weary men,
A hope to make the heart grow young again,
A cry to comrades scattered and afar:
Be constellated, star by circling star;
Give to all mortals justice and forgive:
License must die that liberty may live.
Let Love shine through the fabric of the State—
Love deathless, Love whose other name is Fate.
Fear not: we cannot fail—
The Vision will prevail.
Truth is the Oath of God, and, sure and fast,
Through Death and Hell holds onward to the last.

Art

To Howard Pyle
At her light touch, behold! a voice proceeds
Out of all things to chide our sordid deeds;
A beauty breaks, a beauty ever strange,
The Changeless that is back of all the change.
Lightly it comes as when a rose would be—
Takes feature yet remains a mystery.

On Seeing Vedder's "Pleiades"

I hear a burst of music on the night!
Look at the white whirl of their bodies, see
The sweep of arms seraphical and free,
And over their heads a rush of circling light,
That draws them on with mystery and might:
But O the wild dance and the deathless song,
And O the lifted faces glad and strong—
Eternal passion burning still and white!

But she who glances downward, who is she,
Her face stilled with the shadow of a pain?
The one who let all go for that mad chance?
And does some sudden gust of memory,
Bringing the earth, sweep back into the brain?...
But O the wild white whirl of the wild dance!

The Muse of Labor

And I saw a New Heaven and a New Earth.—St. John.
I come, O heroes, to the world gone wrong;
I bring the hope of nations; and I bear
The warm first rush of rapture in my song,
The faint first light of morning on my hair.
I look upon the ages from a tower;
I am the Muse of the Fraternal State;
No hand can hold me from my crowning hour;
My song is Freedom and my step is Fate.
The toilers go on broken at the heart;
They send the spell of beauty on all lands;
But what avail? the builders have no part—
No share in all the glory of their hands.
I have descended from Alcyone;
I am the muse of Labor and of Mirth;
I come to break the chain of infamy,
That Greed's blind hammers forge about the earth.
I have descended from the Hidden Place,
To make dumb spirits speak and dead feet start:
I feel the wind of battles in my face,
I hear the song of nations in my heart.
I stand by Him, the Hero of the Cross,
To hurl down traitors that misspend His bread;
I touch the star of mystery and loss
To shake the kingdoms of the living dead.
I wear the flower of Christus for a crown;
I poise the suns and give to each a name;
And through the hushed Eternity bend down
To strengthen gods and keep their souls from blame.

I come to overthrow the ancient wrong,
To let the joy of nations rise again;
I am Unselfish Service, I am Song,
I am the Hope that feeds the hearts of men.
I am the Vision in the world-eclipse,
And where I pass the feet of Beauty burn;
And when I set the bugle to my lips,
The youth of work-worn races will return.
I am Religion and the church I build,
Stands on the sacred flesh with passion packed;
In me the ancient gospels are fulfilled—
In me the symbol rises into Fact.
I am the maker of the People's bread,
I bear the little burdens of the day;
Yet in the Mystery of Song I tread
The endless heavens and show the stars their way.

Even Scales

The robber is robbed by his riches;
The tyrant is dragged by his chain;
The schemer is snared by his cunning;
The slayer lies dead by the slain.

Dreyfus

I

A man stood stained! France was one Alp of hate,
Pressing upon him with its iron weight.
In all the circle of the ancient sun,
There was no voice to speak for him—not one.
In all the world of men there was no sound
But of a sword flung broken to the ground.
"'Tis done!" they said, "unless a felon soul
Can tear the leaves out of the Judgment Scroll."
Hell laughed a little season, then behold
How one by one the gates of God unfold!

Swiftly a sword by Unseen Forces hurled,
And then a man rising against the world!

II

Oh, import deep as life is, deep as time!
There is a Something sacred and sublime,
Moving behind the worlds, beyond our ken,
Weighing the stars, weighing the deeds of men.
Take heart, O soul of sorrow, and be strong:
There is One greater than the whole world's wrong.
Be hushed before the high benignant Power
That goes untarrying to the reckoning hour.
O men that forge the fetter, it is vain:
There is a Still Hand stronger than your chain.
'Tis no avail to bargain, sneer, and nod,
And shrug the shoulder for reply to God.
October, .

Memory of Good Deeds

The memory of good deeds will ever stay,
A lamp to light us on the darkened way,
A music to the ear on clamoring street,
A cooling well amid the noonday heat,
A scent of green boughs blown through narrow walls,
A feel of rest when quiet evening falls.

The New Century

While cities rose and blossomed into dust,
While shadowy lines of kings were blown to air,
What was the Purpose brooding on the world,
Through the large leisure of the centuries?
And what the end—failure or victory?
Lo, man has laid his sceptre on the stars,
And sent his spell upon the continents.
The heavens confess their secrets, and the stones,

Silent as God, publish their mystery.
Man calls the lightning from its secret place,
That he may shrink the spaces of the world,
And eavesdrop at the latched Antipodes.
The wild, white, smoking horses of the sea
Are startled by his thunders. The World-Powers
Crowd round to be the lackeys of the king.
His hand has torn the veil of the Great Law,
The law that was before the worlds—before
That far First Whisper on the ancient deep,
The law that swings Arcturus on the North,
And hurls the soul of man upon the way.
But what avail, O builders of the world,
Unless ye build a safety for the soul?
Man has put harness on Leviathan,
And hooks in his incorrigible jaws;
And yet the Perils of the Street remain.
Out of the whirlwind of the cities rise
Lean Hunger and the Worm of Misery,
The heartbreak and the cry of mortal tears.
But hark, the bugles blowing on the peaks;
And hark, a murmur as of many feet,
The cry of captains, the divine alarm!
Look! the last son of Time comes hurrying on,
The strong young Titan of Democracy!
With swinging step he takes the open road,
In love with the winds that beat his hairy breast.
Baring his sunburnt strength to all the world,
He casts his eyes abroad with Jovian glance—
Searches the tracks of old Tradition; scans
With rebel heart the Book of Pedigree;
Peers into the face of Privilege and cries,
"Why are you halting in the path of man?
Is it your shoulder bears the human load?
Do you draw down the rains of the sweet heaven,
And keep the green things growing? Back to hell!"
God is descending from eternity,
And all things, good and evil, build the road.

Yea, down in the thick of things, the men of greed
Are thumping the inhospitable clay.
By wondrous toils the men without the Dream,
Led onward by a something unawares,
Are laying the foundations of the Dream,
The Kingdom of Fraternity foretold.

The Need of the Hour

Fling forth the triple-colored flag to dare
The bright, untraveled highways of the air.
Blow the undaunted bugles, blow, and yet
Let not the boast betray us to forget.
Lo, there are high adventures for this hour—
Tourneys to test the sinews of our power.
For we must parry—as the years increase—
The hazards of success, the risks of peace!
What do we need to keep the nation whole,
To guard the pillars of the State? We need
The fine audacities of honest deed;
The homely old integrities of soul;
The swift temerities that take the part
Of outcast right—the wisdom of the heart;
Brave hopes that Mammon never can detain,
Nor sully with his gainless clutch for gain.
We need the Cromwell fire to make us feel
The common burden and the public trust
To be a thing as sacred and august
As the white vigil where the angels kneel.
We need the faith to go a path untrod,
The power to be alone and vote with God.

The Lizard

I sit among the hoary trees
With Aristotle on my knees,
And turn with serious hand the pages,
Lost in the cobweb-hush of ages;

When suddenly with no more sound
Than any sunbeam on the ground,
The little hermit of the place
Is peering up into my face—
The slim gray hermit of the rocks,
With bright inquisitive, quick eyes,
His life a round of harks and shocks,
A little ripple of surprise.
Now lifted up, intense and still,
Sprung from the silence of the hill
He hangs upon the ledge a-glisten,
And his whole body seems to listen!
My pages give a little start,
And he is gone! to be a part
Of the old cedar's crumpled bark,
A mottled scar, a weather-mark!
How halt am I, how mean of birth,
Beside this darting pulse of earth!
I only have the wit to look
Into a big presumptuous book,
To find some sage's rigid plan
To tell me how to be a man.
Tradition lays its dead hand cold
Upon our youth—and we are old.
But this wise hermit, this gray friar,
He has no law but heart's desire.
He somehow touches higher truth,
The circle of eternal youth.

The Humming Bird

A sudden whir of eager sound—
And now a something throbs around
The flowers that watch the fountain. Look!
It touched the rose, the green leaves shook,
I think, and yet so lightly tost
That not a spark of dew was lost.
Tell me, O Rose, what thing it is

That now appears, now vanishes?
Surely it took its fire-green hue
From daybreaks that it glittered through;
Quick, for this sparkle of the dawn
Glints through the garden and is gone.
What was the message, Rose, what word;
Delight foretold, or hope deferred?

The Round-Up

Down, down the wild canyons we go in a flurry;
The cedars sweep by in their mystical hurry;
Gone into the wind are the languor and worry—
Gone into the west with the phantom moon.
Ho! there is the lord of the hills and the valleys;
It is he that leads in the midsummer sallies
High into the steeps where the gray chaparral is;
It is he that leads to the low lagoon.
Where the wild mustard splashes the slope with yellow,
He has turned at bay—ah, the powerful fellow!
See the toss of his head—hear the breath and the bellow;
How he tears the ground with his angry hoofs!
Now he breaks a wild path through the deep, plumy rushes,
(A loud bird high on a tamarack hushes)
Right on through a glory of crimson he crushes,
On into the gloom under leafy roofs.
Oh, the joy of the wind in our faces! We follow
The cattle—we shout down the poppy-hung hollow.
Lo! out of the cliff we have startled a swallow,
And startled the echoes on rocky fells.
Ho! what was it passed? Were they leaves—were they sparrows
That whispered away like a hurtle of arrows?
The rose-odor thickens—the deep gorge narrows;
Now the herd takes down through the scented dells.
Speed, speed, leave the brooks to their potter and prattle;
Sweep on with the thunder and surge of the cattle,
The hurry, the voices, the keen joy of battle—
The hills and the wind and the open light.

Now on into camp by the sycamores yonder;
Now o'er the guitar let the light fingers wander;
Let thoughts in the high heart grow pensive and fonder;
Then stars and the dream of a summer night.

Song of the Fay

My life is a dream, a dream,
In the moon's cool beam;
Some day I shall wake and desire
A touch of the infinite fire.
But now 'tis enough that I be
In the light on the sea;
Enough that I climb with the cloud
When the winds of the morning are loud;
Enough that I fade with my star
When the doors of the East unbar.
My life is a long delight
In the wonder of night.
I quiet the heart of the rose
When she quakes at the thought of the snows;
I count the blown leaves of the Fall,
And I comfort them all.
Sometimes I awake with a start
In the song of a poet's heart.
Some day I shall know life whole—
Shall suffer and find me a soul.

The World-Purpose

Men sadly say that Love's high dream is vain,
That one force holds the heart—the hope of gain.
Are, then, the August Powers behind the veil
Weary of watch and powerless to prevail?
Have they grown palsied with the creep of age,
And do they burn no more with pallid rage?
Are the shrines empty and the altars cold,
Where once the saints and heroes knelt of old?

Not so: the vast in-brothering of man—
The glory of the universe—began
When first the heart of the Mother Darkness heard
The Whisper, and the ancient chaos stirred.
Ever the feet of Christ were in events,
Bridging the seas, shaking the continents.
His feet are heard in the historic march
Under the whirlwind, under the starry arch.
Forever the Great Purpose presses on,
From darkness unto darkness, dawn to dawn,
Resolved to lay the rafter and the beam
Of Justice—the imperishable Dream.
This is the voice of Time against the Hours;
This is the witness of the Cosmic Powers;
This is the Music of the Ages—this
The song whose first note broke the First Abyss.
All that we glory in was once a dream;
The World-Will marches onward, gleam by gleam.
New voices speak, dead paths begin to stir:
Man is emerging from the sepulchre!
Let no man dare, let no man ever dare
To mark on Time's great way, "No Thoroughfare!"

To Young America

In spite of the stare of the wise and the world's derision,
Dare travel the star-blazed road, dare follow the Vision.
It breaks as a hush on the soul in the wonder of youth;
And the lyrical dream of the boy is the kingly truth.
The world is a vapor, and only the Vision is real—
Yea, nothing can hold against Hell but the Wingèd Ideal.

The Brown o' the Year

What would you speak with that visage old,
O cliff by the windy shore?
What passion that never a song could hold—
What word of the Nevermore?

What would you tell with that silent look,
O bleak, bare oak by the way?
Earth's grief is all in that bough that shook,
That leaf that could not stay.

Wind of the Fall

I hear that wail in the windy pine
And I suddenly know:
It wakes in my heart a dream divine
And a sacred woe.
I heard that cry from your spirit then,
O wind of the Fall!
I, too, have carried the grief of men;
I have felt it all.

The Free Press

Hail, young Prometheus, risen again to Time,
The friend of man and foeman of man's Foe!
Climb the new heavens and seize the nobler fire.
Still teach the wisdom of the plough and loom,
The sweetness of the threshold and the hearth.
Be to the sower of the field a sign
To point the circuits of the frost, a voice
To cry the coming of the hurricane.
Be to the scholar, by his waning lamp,
A bringer of the tidings of the stars,
News of the forces and the frame of things.
Be to the poet, leagued with Death and Eld,
A Memnon whisper of the Mystery,
Life's lofty joy and immemorial grief.
Be to the calm historian a glass
Where, through the rush of phantoms, he can see
The majesty and quietness of Truth,
The craft of God, the lure and threat of Time.
Hail, Titan, with the hair upon your breast!
Be terrible in battle to throw down

The stronghold of the traitors and their crew.
Flash down the sky-born lightnings of the Pen;
Let loose the cramped-up thunders of the Types.
Hurl on the Jupiter of Greed enthroned
Defiance, endless challenge, fire of scorn.
Stand out upon the walls of darkness—stand
A young god with a bugle at his lips
To rouse the watchmen sleeping on their towers.
Fling out the banner of the People's Right—
A flag in love with all the winds of heaven;
Plunge your dread sword into the Spoiler's den;
Hurl down into the faces of the thieves
The blaze of its intolerable light....
Fail not, for in your failure Freedom fails!

A Bargain

Scoffer, you cry, "Where is your 'other world,'
Your fabled heaven in far eternities?"
Well said, but first, before your lip is curled,
Tell ('tis a little thing) where this world is!

"Inasmuch...."

Wild tempest swirled on Moscow's castled height;
Wild sleet shot slanting down the wind of night;
Quick snarling mouths from out the darkness sprang
To strike you in the face with tooth and fang.
Javelins of ice hung on the roofs of all;
The very stones were aching in the wall,
Where Ivan stood a watchman on his hour,
Guarding the Kremlin by the northern tower,
When, lo! a half-bare beggar tottered past,
Shrunk up and stiffened in the bitter blast.
A heap of misery he drifted by,
And from the heap came out a broken cry.
At this the watchman straightened with a start;
A tender grief was tugging at his heart,

The thought of his dead father, bent and old
And lying lonesome in the ground so cold.
Then cried the watchman starting from his post:
"Little father, this is yours; you need it most!"
And tearing off his hairy coat, he ran
And wrapt it warm around the beggar man.
That night the piling snows began to fall,
And the good watchman died beside the wall.
But waking in the Better Land that lies
Beyond the reaches of these cooping skies,
Behold, the Lord came out to greet him home,
Wearing the coat he gave by Moscow's dome—
Wearing the hairy heavy coat he gave
By Moscow's tower before he felt the grave!
And Ivan, by the old Earth-memory stirred,
Cried softly with a wonder in his word:
"And where, dear Lord, found you this coat of mine,
A thing unfit for glory such as Thine?"
Then the Lord answered with a look of light:
"This coat, My son, you gave to Me last night."

"The Father's Business"

Who puts back into place a fallen bar,
Or flings a rock out of a traveled road,
His feet are moving toward the central star,
His name is whispered in the God's abode.

A Guard of the Sepulchre

Behold, some of the watch came into the city and told unto the Chief Priests all the things that were come to pass, and ... they gave large money unto the soldiers, saying: Say, His disciples came by night and stole Him away while we slept.—Matthew.

I was a Roman soldier in my prime;
Now age is on me and the yoke of time.
I saw your Risen Christ, for I am he

Who reached the hyssop to Him on the tree;
And I am one of two who watched beside
The Sepulchre of Him we crucified.
All that last night I watched with sleepless eyes;
Great stars arose and crept across the skies.
The world was all too still for mortal rest,
For pitiless thoughts were busy in the breast.
The night was long, so long, it seemed at last
I had grown old and a long life had passed.
Far off the hills of Moab, touched with light,
Were swimming in the hollow of the night.
I saw Jerusalem all wrapped in cloud,
Stretched like a dead thing folded in a shroud.
Once in the pauses of our whispered talk,
I heard a something on the garden walk.
Perhaps it was a crisp leaf lightly stirred—
Perhaps the dream-note of a waking bird.
Then suddenly an angel burning white
Came down with earthquake in the breaking light,
And rolled the great stone from the Sepulchre,
Mixing the morning with a scent of myrrh.
And lo, the Dead had risen with the day:
The Man of Mystery had gone His way!
Years have I wandered, carrying my shame;
Now let the Tooth of Time eat out my name.
For we, who all the Wonder might have told,
Kept silence, for our mouths were stopt with gold.

The Song of the Shepherds

And the shepherds returned, glorifying and praising God for all the things that they had heard and seen.—Luke.

It was near the first cock-crowing,
And Orion's wheel was going,
When an angel stood before us and our hearts were sore afraid.
Lo, his face was like the lightning,
When the walls of heaven are whitening,

And he brought us wondrous tidings of a joy that shall not fade.
Then a Splendor shone around us,
In the still field where he found us,
A-watch upon the Shepherd Tower and waiting for the light;
There where David as a stripling,
Saw the ewes and lambs go rippling
Down the little hills and hollows at the falling of the night.
Oh, what tender, sudden faces
Filled the old familiar places,
The barley-fields where Ruth of old went gleaning with the birds!

Down the skies the host came swirling,
Like sea-waters white and whirling,
And our hearts were strangely shaken by the wonder of their words.
Haste, O people: all are bidden—
Haste from places, high or hidden:
In Mary's Child the Kingdom comes, the heaven in beauty bends!
He has made all life completer:
He has made the Plain Way sweeter,
For the stall is His first shelter and the cattle His first friends.
He has come! the skies are telling:
He has quit the glorious dwelling;
And first the tidings came to us, the humble shepherd folk.
He has come to field and manger,
And no more is God a Stranger:
He comes as Common Man at home with cart and crookèd yoke.
As the shadow of a cedar
To a traveller in gray Kedar
Will be the kingdom of His love, the kingdom without end.
Tongues and Ages may disclaim Him,
Yet the Heaven of heavens will name Him
Lord of peoples, Light of nations, elder Brother, tender Friend.

The Prince of Whim

Borne on like a bubble
In bright little trouble
My elf child glimmers and goes;
As glad as a throstle
Whose tremolos jostle
The rain on the leaf of a rose.
He comes in a twinkling,
With never an inkling
That law is not one with his word;
But gives me good wages,
The penny of ages—
Love wild as the heart of a bird.
He laughs down my quiet,
This lord of the riot,
This Prince of the Kingdom of Whim;
The world is his castle,
And I am his vassal
To trumpet the triumphs of him!

The Plowman

His furrows are darkening into the hollow,
Lightly behind him the blackbirds follow—
By quick little journeys they follow and whistle.
Now a gossamer ship breaks away to the blue
(Who stands by the railing and waves adieu?)
All night it was moored to a thistle.
Who knows the glad business afoot on the by-way?
Who know the bold hopes sent adrift on the skyway?

Song's Eternity

Into the song of the Poet are built the things that endure:
The Pillars of Karnak will crumble but the song of Shelley is sure.
It will hold through the ages of ages, like the heavens steadied in air:

The hoofs that trample the kingdoms down that miracle must spare.

The God of Song and Mirth

'Twas the God of Song and Mirth
Who descended to the Earth.
It was He who veiled His face
In the sorrow of the race;
He who toiled at Nazareth,
Going with us down to death;
He who bowed the heavens for men,
And arose to light again.
'Twas the First-born Son of Light
Shone upon the human night,
Bringing down the Final Truth
In His deep, eternal youth.
God was reconciled to man
When the ages first began;
But that man be reconciled
God became a little child.
So appeared the God of Song
In the planet going wrong;
So appeared the God of Light,
God of Passion still and white;
Came to help us lift the weight
Of the planetary fate;
Came and taught the one relief
For the gray primeval grief—
Taught that Love, though deified,
Could not set the Law aside.

St. Elizabeth of Hungary

I think of that friend of the people that lady of long ago,
That high-born dame of Hungary who felt the common woe—
Who loved the work-worn multitude whose pillow is a stone,
And felt beat in upon her heart their sorrow as her own.

She bent to lift, for in her blood ran some heroic strain
Of simple serving majesty strayed down from Charlemagne.
Queen of a hundred legends, star of a misty past,
While cities rise and cities fade, her memory will last.
It was upon a Christmas eve, and all the world was white
With snow that sent an awesome hush on hollow and on height;
And green boughs bended with hoar weight, and under them the birds
Huddled together, making friends with little hornèd herds.
And far from soundless gorges in the soundless forest deep,
The wild boar humped up closer in the hollow of his heap;
And workers huddled in their huts among the stiffened trees,
The doorstones blue with ice, the eaves with frosty filigrees.
And Horsel's peak hung ghostly still upon the wintry sky,
But Wartburg's castle-hall was filled with many a joyous cry,
With hurrying feet and merry fleer of scullion, churl, and maid,
For now within a happy hour the banquet must be laid.
Pert pages in their purfled shoes went twinkling in and out,
And from the towers came snatch of song and many a ruddy shout.
Elizabeth was there above, among her maiden band,
Spinning the new-cut wool to warm the naked of her land.
(O serving queen, I honor thee—queen of a day gone down,
Who carried dimly in thy heart the meaning of the crown!)
And now the steward gave a sign, and on the frosty moats
The sceptered heralds blew again their crisp and crinkling notes.
There fell a momentary hush upon the corridors;
Then stir of feet, then whisper of silk gowns across the floors
Came onward like the tumult of white barley in the breeze;
Then young Elizabeth the Moon, leading her Pleiades!
Their robes were shot with thread of gold that into blossom broke,
And jewels darkling in their hair at every motion woke—
Yolinda, Bertrade, Thekla, Brune, Bertilla, Hildegarde,
And Kinga, tallest of the seven, and by her side the bard,
Gray Vogelweide, the lyric swan, telling with flash of youth,
How once he stood against the world for Hungary and truth—
How singing in this knightly hall, circled by courtly throng,

He fought the star of Austria in Wartburg's War of Song.
Then the young sovereign Lewis and his guests swept glowing in—
Lord, liegeman, shaggy baron, gallant knight and paladin,
Each with a winsome lady and a wreath of storied days:
Dark Rudolph home from Holy War with Lion Richard's praise;
Walter the Falconer, and Franz, the flower of Hesse's men,
Who brought Elizabeth a sword torn from a Saracen;
Hellgraf with jewelled glove agleam high in his helmet's hold,
A glove she gave a beggar once and he bought back with gold.
And so the throng came eddying in, and with the splendor went
Ripple of silver laughter and of whispered compliment.
The torches flamed and faltered, sending up white whirls of smoke,
To hang as twilight in the roof raftered with crookèd oak.
Up from the chimney log the notes of many woodlands sang;
Quick through the flame the colors of a hundred summers sprang.
The blaze threw on the arrased wall a gush of golden light,
Where hung Saint Stephen's shield between two angels in still flight,
Forever moving upward toward the cherubs overhead,
Now sinking into shade and now breaking to rosy red.
A swinging door, a spicy smell, and beaming Hugolin
With smoking boar's head lifted high came proudly panting in.
And as the sparkling feast went on the board began to stir
With talk of knightly valor and the Holy Sepulchre,
With prattle of the tidings from Jerusalem and Rome;
But sweet Elizabeth, her thoughts were not so far from home.
In spite of rosy radiance, in spite of trumpet calls,
The Sorrow of the People sent its shadow through the walls.
For sitting there beside her lord a sudden silence came
Upon her soul, and all the voices and the horn's acclaim
Died; and the glowing pageant broke and faded into air,
And only the faces of the poor whose tables are so bare
Pressed in upon her soul that night, pressed in that gala night;
Only the toilers' cheerless homes rose on her inward sight.
And then a graver thought let in a darkness on her heart—

A thought of all the feasts they spread of which they have no part—
A thought, too, of this splendor on this holy Christmas eve,
A splendor wrung from toiling hands by those that tax and thieve.
Of all those fragrant dishes only two would not profane;
Only the bread and water there had come of honest gain;
These only were not pilfered from the toiler's lean supply;
And these she took with happy hands, but let the rest go by.
And so the table roared away into the winter night,
Until the toasts went round the board with laughter at the height.
They drank to saints and prophets old, to Peter and Isadore,
To Stephen, Vincent, Boniface, and to a dozen more.
Then valiant Wolfram in his turn upstarted with a cry:
"Drink to Archangel Michael, that good fighter in the sky,
That prince of God that all the hosts of Satan could not tame!"
Up to their feet the feasters sprang at that great angel's name.
Clinking their cups from side to side, they made, in the torches' flare,
The sign of the cross with their jewelled cups high flashing in the air.
Now cried the duke: "Not all the saints have felt the wind of death;
Come, drink to one who walks the Earth, my wife Elizabeth;
And I will pledge her beauty with this water in her cup."
So stooping down he caught and swung her golden goblet up,
And tasted—paused—tasted again, for lo, it was rare wine!
More strangely sweet than any juice pressed from an earthly vine.
"Ho, varlet, from what pipe this wine and from what cellar shelf?"
"From good Saint Kilian's well, sire, and I drew it up myself!"
She flushed; the table stared; the duke looked foolishly about,
The hall so still they heard far bells breaking the night without.
Then up spake Helias the Seer: "I saw the water poured—
Saw, too, an angel bending by our lady at the board,
Pouring with courteous gesture from a flagon of red wine,

Then fading in the brightness of the firelight's dancing shine."
She heard in glad amaze: he wins God's favor unawares
Who, self-forgot in brother love, a brother's burden bears.

*   *   *   *   *

And this seven centuries ago. And now her sainted feet
Are on the fields of Paradise, making its old paths sweet.
And there she has her fill of love where the Friendly City is,
Her warm hands white with labor in God's busy palaces.

The Joy-Maker

Time's touch can dim our sorrows and destroy,
But only Art can turn them into joy.

The Face of Life

An Adaptation.
Life cried to Youth, "I bear the cryptic key:
I grant you two desires, but only two.
What gifts have I to crown and comfort you?"
Youth answered, "I am blind and I would see;
Open my eyes and let me look on thee."
'Twas done: he saw the face of Life, and then
Cried brokenly, "Now make me blind again!"

The Story of Bacchus

A Grecian legend
What boy with his face to the Ægean Sea
Went threading his way over mountain and plain,
With a spirit as glad as a blossoming tree?
It was Bacchus, now pure as the wild white rain,
But soon to be worshiped by mortals, with passion and sorrow and pain.
He had found a vine on the forest ways,
And a skeleton bird in a rocky pass
To shelter the leaf from the sunny rays;
But it grew till he sheltered them both, alas,

In the hollow skull of a lion, and then in the skull of an ass!
As he lay at noon in a mossy rest,
The vine had shot up all a-tremble with light.
Now he bears it home—(O the doom unguessed!)
On, on, while the hills swing away out of sight—
Till the misty far mountains rise dimly, and pass in a silent flight.
At last when his garden was furrowed, he found
That the bones were all twined by the lusty root;
So he planted the whole in the deep-stirred ground,
And lightly danced to his Lydian flute,
While the leafy depths of the eerie vine purpled with clustering fruit.
Then he made him wine—for it was the grape—
And darkened its depths with a perilous spell,
And gave it to man with the angel shape,
When lo! a wonder and terror befell—
Was it a wonder from Heaven—was it a terror from Hell?
For he drinks—and he carols and sings like a bird!
And drinking again of the magical glass,
He is proud as a lion when passion-stirred!
But drinking once more of the liquor, alas,
He loses the shape of the angel, and takes on the shape of an ass!

Lost Lands

I mind me once in boyhood when the mist
Swirled round me, ash of pearl and amethyst,
How, in an unknown, difficult, high place,
I pushed the green boughs backward from my face,
And with a fire along the blood, a cry,
Rode out upon a headland in the sky.
I know not in what world it was—Mirak
Or Algol, or some further Zodiac!
I looked down on a sea of fog below;
Saw strange lands rise, strange waters furl and flow,
Breaking on newly lifted reefs and shores—
New Africas, new Indies, new Azores—
Lands that allured me to illustrious deed,

Past Roland's fame, and all his knightly breed—
Fringes of lands no foot had ever found,
Where billows climbed and burst without a sound;
While further still, on dim untraveled seas,
Gleamed lost Atlantis, lost Hesperides.

Poet-Lore

The poet is forever young
And speaks the one immortal tongue.
To him the wonder never dies,
For youth is looking through his eyes.
Pale listener at the heart of things,
He hears the voices and the wings:
He hears the skylark overhead—
Hears the far footfalls of the dead.
When the swift Muses seize their child,
Then God has gladness rich and wild;
For when the bard is caught and hurled,
A splendor breaks across the world.
His song distils a saving power
From foot-worn stone, from wayside flower.
He knows the gospel of the trees,
The whispered message of the seas;
Finds in some beetle on the road
A power to lift the human load;
Sees, in some dead leaf dried and curled,
The deeper meaning of the world;
Hears through the roar of mortal things
The God's immortal whisperings;
Sees the world-wonder rise and fall,
And knows that Beauty made it all.
He walks the circle of the sun,
And sees the bright Powers laugh and run.
He feels the motion of the sphere,
And builds his song in sacred fear.
He finds the faithful witness hid
In poppy-head and Pyramid.

The Golden Heaven or the Pit—
He shakes the music out of it.
All things yield up their souls to him
From dateless dust to seraphim.

The Hindered Guest

Friar Hilary, of Barbizon,
(Rest to his soul where his soul has gone!)
Was a man whose life was long perplexed
By pious juggles with the text.
The logic of St. Thomas' books
Was fastened to his mind with hooks.
He knew Tertullian's work complete—
That treatise on the Paraclete.
He knew the words Chrysostom hurled
In golden thunder on the world;
And he could commentate and quote
The thirteen books Saint Cyril wrote.
The controversies of Jerome,
He could recite them, tome by tome.
The friar was tall and spare and spent,
Like a cedar of Lebanon bare and bent.
His eyes were sunken and burned too bright,
Like restless stars in the pit of night.
The friar had built a tower of stone,
And dwelt far up in a cell alone;
And from the turret, gray in air,
He called to God with psalm and prayer,
To come as he did to the wise of old—
To come as the ancient voice foretold.
All day the hawk swung overhead;
All day the holy page was read.
One bleak December he fasted sore,
That Christ might knock at his low door—
Lord Jesus shine across the floor.
For he was hungry to be fed
With the holy love, with the mystic bread.

Yet Christ came not to sup with him,
And Christmas Eve fell chilly and dim.
"Where art Thou?" he would cry and hark,
While echoes answered in the dark....
Where was the Lord—was he afar,
Throned calmly on the central star?
Now suddenly there came a cry
As of a mortal like to die.
Up sprang the friar, the doors of oak
He flung asunder at a stroke.
Down stair by stair his quick feet flew,
Startling the owls that the rafters knew,
Breaking the webs that barred the way,
Crushing the mosses that fear the day.
Into the pitiless street he ran
To find a stricken fellow-man,
And carry him in upon his breast,
With many a halt on the stairs for rest.
He washed the feet and stroked the hair,
And for the once forgot his prayer.
He gave him wine that the Pope had sent
For some great day of the Sacrament;
And looking up, behold, at his side
Was bending also the Crucified!
He had come at last to the lonesome place,
And standing there with a courteous grace,
Threw sainted light on the friar's face.
And then the Master said: "My son,
My children on my errands run;
And when you flung the psalter by
And hurried to a brother's cry,
You turned at last your rusty key,
And left the door ajar for Me."

Supplication

Give me heart-touch with all that live,
And strength to speak my word;

But if that is denied me, give
The strength to live unheard.
[THE END]